OK...
THE RIV...

BY ADAM BLADE

ORCHARD

OKAWA
THE RIVER BEAST

With special thanks to Michael Ford
To Lachlan Evans, a special boy

ORCHARD BOOKS

First published in Great Britain in 2014 by Orchard Books
This edition published in 2016 by The Watts Publishing Group

5 7 9 10 8 6 4

Text © 2014 Beast Quest Limited.
Cover and inside illustrations by Steve Sims
© Beast Quest Limited 2014

Illustrations copyright Orchard Books, 2014

Beast Quest is a registered trademark of Beast Quest Limited
Series created by Beast Quest Limited, London

The moral rights of the author and illustrator have been asserted.
All characters and events in this publication, other than those clearly in the public domain,
are fictitious and any resemblance to real persons, living or dead, is purely coincidental.

A CIP catalogue record for this book is available from the British Library.

ISBN 978 1 40832 928 3

Printed and bound by CPI Group (UK) Ltd, Croydon, CR0 4YY

The paper and board used in this book are made from wood from responsible sources

Orchard Books
An imprint of Hachette Children's Group
Part of The Watts Publishing Group Limited
Carmelite House, 50 Victoria Embankment, London EC4Y 0DZ

An Hachette UK Company
www.hachette.co.uk
www.hachettechildrens.co.uk

STORY ONE

Greetings, followers of the Quests,

It is a strange time in the kingdom of Avantia. The Beasts are no longer a secret – now, every person in the kingdom knows we have magical protectors...

...and magical enemies. Tom may have vanquished Malvel, and defeated the treacherous Judge, but I cannot relax. Evil surely still lurks in the shadows, ready to rise up and attack the kingdom once again. We must always be prepared.

I hope that I am being too cautious...

Daltec, Wizard of Avantia

CHAPTER ONE

CELEBRATION

Tom thrust a spare tunic into his knapsack, along with a water flask, some strips of dried meat, a slab of cheese and a couple of apples. He looked around his bedchamber in King Hugo's palace, making sure he hadn't forgotten anything. *A blanket – of course!* Their destination was several days' ride away, and they'd be sleeping under the stars. Nights in

Avantia could be very cold indeed.

His eyes fell on his shield and sword, leaning against the wall near the door. He would never forget those.

Hopefully I won't need them, though.

He was not heading out on a Quest this time. Far from it – his uncle Henry's fifty-second birthday was in three days' time, and Tom planned to surprise him by turning up for the party. Only Aunt Maria knew he was coming – she'd written to the palace and told Tom how much it would mean to his uncle. Tom had been unsure at first – what if Kensa or Sanpao or another enemy attacked Avantia? What if there were Beasts to face?

But King Hugo had insisted that Tom deserved a holiday.

"If we need you, we'll send word," he'd said.

Tom heard urgent footsteps on the stairs outside his room. His heart began to thump, and he rushed to grab his sword.

There must be trouble in the kingdom…

Elenna burst into the room, a grin on her face, and Tom's heart stilled.

"Aren't you ready yet?" she asked.

Tom laughed and fastened his sword belt. "I am now. Let's go!"

As they made their way to the stables, Elenna's wolf, Silver, scampered out from the shade of a wall and joined them. His tail wagged with excitement.

Tom went to a stall and led out his black stallion, Storm. The stable lad had already put the saddle on, but Tom tightened the straps. *Just in case we have to gallop.* He looped his knapsack over the saddle and patted Storm's neck.

"Ready for an adventure, old friend? It's a long ride, but Aunt Maria's sure to spoil you with lots of

14

carrots when we get to Errinel!"

"We could just ask Daltec to magic us there," said Elenna. "His spells are getting much better." She smiled. "If anyone's earned the right *not* to slog for miles, it's us!"

Tom swung himself into the saddle. "I don't like using magic unless we have to," he said. "Remember our first Quest. We didn't use magic then, did we? It was just the four of us."

"I suppose you're right," said Elenna, climbing onto Storm's back behind Tom.

They trotted across the palace courtyard. As they did so, a plump woman bustled across the cobbles towards them. It was Audrey, from the kitchens. She held out a stoppered flagon.

"Young Tom!" she cried. "You

almost forgot this."

Tom reached down and took the flagon. "Of course!" he said. "Thank you, Audrey."

"What is it?" Elenna asked.

"The City's finest fruit punch," said Tom. "A gift for my uncle from King Hugo." He took out the stopper, and a wonderful fruity aroma rose to his nostrils. He held it to Elenna for a sniff.

"Mmm," she said. "He'll love it, I'm sure."

"Ride safely, both of you," said Audrey, hurrying back to the kitchens. Tom stowed the flask carefully at the top of his knapsack. He was determined not to spill a drop of the punch.

Daltec the Wizard was waiting for them at the palace gates. He reached out to stroke Storm's nose, but his face was lined with worry.

"What's the matter?" asked Tom.

Daltec looked at his feet. "I've got a

bad feeling about your trip to Errinel, Tom," he said. "Maybe…maybe you shouldn't go?"

Tom's grip tightened on the reins. He'd learned long ago always to listen to a Wizard's concerns.

"Tell us what you're worried about," he said.

Daltec shrugged. "My crystal ball is clear, and there have been no sightings of our enemies. It's just a feeling."

Elenna shifted in the saddle behind him, and Tom could tell she was impatient to get going. *Maybe Daltec's worrying unnecessarily*, he thought. *I can't let my aunt down just because of a hunch.*

"You know where we'll be," he said to Daltec. "If there's *any* sign of trouble, come and find us in Errinel."

The Wizard nodded, his jaw tight, and Tom nudged Storm through the gates. They were off at last!

CHAPTER TWO

A STRANGE ENCOUNTER

The day had passed without incident.
It was nice to ride through the
kingdom, greeting farmers in the
fields and travellers on the road, with
no thought of danger. When night
fell, they made camp on the edge of a
wild orchard, just off the main track.
There was enough old wood to build
a fire and make a soup of nettles.

Tom took the flagon from his knapsack and placed it upright at the bottom of the nearest tree. Nothing had spilled so far. As he folded his spare tunic to make a pillow, he couldn't shake the memory of Daltec's anxious face. Perhaps he should have trusted the Wizard's instincts. But as he lay under his blanket, staring at the stars through the branches of the tree above, everything seemed peaceful and calm.

Elenna lay down on the other side of their fire, and from her slow, regular breathing, Tom knew she was asleep. *I should sleep too*, thought Tom. *It'll be a long day tomorrow.*

Storm stood off to one side, hitched to a tree trunk. Silver slept beside the horse's hooves, ears flat.

His hearing is better than ours, Tom

thought. *If there's any danger, Silver will sense it.*

Tom looked into the crackling flames of the fire and willed his limbs to relax. He thought of how delighted Uncle Henry would be with his punch. Soon he felt sleep tugging at his eyelids...

"Wake up!" said Elenna.

Tom sat up with a jolt. "What?" he said, reaching for his sword.

His friend was already sitting, eyes darting around. Tom looked behind him and saw that Silver's ears were up. From the dying embers in the campfire he guessed they had not been asleep that long.

"I heard something," said Elenna, her eyes bright in the moonlight.

Tom jumped to his feet, scanning the darkness of the orchard. The trees looked different now – grey shadows standing silently, their branches like knotted fingers grasping at the sky. A light breeze made their leaves tremble.

Elenna had an arrow at her bowstring already.

Then Tom heard something too – heavy breathing, broken footsteps… coming their way. He drew his sword quickly and looked through the trees towards the road.

A small, bent figure shambled towards them, and Tom relaxed. From the long grey hair covering most of her face, Tom could see it was an old woman. He noticed her limping, and wondered if she'd fallen on the road.

Tom slid his sword back into his scabbard and ran forward, catching the woman just as she tripped and fell. "It's all right," he said. "I've got you."

"Th-thank you," she said weakly.

"Don't talk," said Tom, as he guided her towards the fire. She felt as light

as a small child.

"Bandits!" The old woman gripped his arm with one thin hand, and pointed back towards the road with the other. "Bandits attacked me! They stole my possessions. Thank goodness I saw the glow of your fire. I managed to escape…"

"Stay calm," said Tom. "I'll have a look." He nodded to Elenna, who took the woman's hands, then he drew his sword and ran towards the trees. There hadn't been reports of robbers on the road for a long time – Captain Harkman's patrols had arrested many and scared the rest away.

At the road he scanned north and south. There was no sign of anyone. In the soft light of the moon he looked at the track's surface, but could see only one set of prints in the dust – the old woman's.

"Strange," he muttered. He walked a few paces, searching for clues. If he could find the bandits' tracks he could follow them. No one could be allowed to terrorise travellers on Avantia's roads.

"Tom, come quickly!" Elenna cried.

He rushed back to the camp, and found Elenna crouching over the old woman. She was lying prone on the floor.

"She collapsed," said Elenna.

Tom kneeled beside her. "Maybe the bandits hit her head," he said, trying to move the long hair off her face to search for a wound.

The old woman stirred and batted his hand away. "I'm fine," she croaked. "It was just a dizzy spell."

Elenna offered her a flask of water, and the old woman drank deeply, facing away from them. "Thank you for your kindness," she said, sounding stronger. "May I ask one more favour?"

"Of course," said Tom.

The old woman turned back to them, but sat hunched over. "Let me stay beside your fire tonight. I fear to go back on the road on my own."

Tom smiled, and offered her his tunic-pillow and blanket. "Take these," he said.

Elenna piled more dry wood onto the embers and soon it caught light.

Tom watched the old woman lie down stiffly and pull the blanket up to her chin. He decided to sleep sitting up against a tree, and settled himself in among the gnarled roots. It didn't

take long to fall asleep this time.

Tom woke, shivering, as a grey dawn
spread across the night sky. At once
he remembered the old woman. He
glanced around and saw his spare

tunic on the ground, neatly folded.

The old woman had gone.

Tom sat up, throwing off the blanket. *I hope the rest of her journey is a safe one, wherever she's going.*

He prodded Elenna's shoulder, and she opened her eyes sleepily.

"We need to keep moving," Tom said.

As he packed his belongings away and fed Storm an apple, he saw that his flagon of punch had fallen over. In a panic, he ran to pick it up, relieved to feel its weight. None of the

contents had spilled out.

He tightened the loose stopper.

If that's the worst thing that happens on this journey, I'll be very happy indeed.

CHAPTER THREE

HOMECOMING

Two days later, Tom and Elenna saw the smoke of Errinel's chimneys ahead of them.

"I bet it feels good to be home," said Elenna.

Tom couldn't help the broad smile spreading across his lips. He guided Storm around the back of the houses towards the village stables, trying to stay out of sight. The first villager

they came across was Terrence, the
boy who looked after the stables. He
could only have been seven years old,
and his eyes widened when he saw
Tom, who put a finger to his lips.

"Can you look after Storm for
me?" Tom said. "We're here for the
birthday party." Terrence nodded and

took Storm's reins, marvelling at the huge horse.

Tom and Elenna made their way towards Uncle Henry's forge, Silver loping along beside them. Through the gaps between the houses, Tom could see long tables being set up in the main square. Villagers were up ladders tying coloured bunting to the eaves of the houses, and a stage had been set up for Errinel's musicians.

Soon Tom heard the rhythmic *clang* of a hammer on metal. They followed the sound to his uncle's house. *Of course Henry is hard at work, even on his birthday!* Tom peered around the door into the forge. Uncle Henry was bent over the anvil, his brawny arm moving up and down as he hammered at a piece of glowing metal. Sparks flew off with each blow, landing on his skin, but Henry liked to boast he no longer felt them.

Henry set down his hammer and, using tongs, plunged the metal into a water bath with a sizzle. Steam billowed up, and when he withdrew the object with the tongs, Tom saw it was an axe-head, perfectly crafted.

"Happy birthday!" Tom called.

Henry spun around, his mouth gaping in shock for a heartbeat. Then he grinned. He tossed aside the axe-head and rushed to Tom, opening his arms wide. Tom hugged him.

"I had no idea you were coming," said Henry.

"After Aunt Maria wrote to me," said Tom, "I couldn't miss this!"

His uncle released him from the bear hug, but still gripped Tom's shoulders as he grinned at him. "I

knew she was keeping a secret from me," he said. "She's barely been able to look me in the eye all morning."

He looked past Tom. "And Elenna, too!"

"Hello, Henry," said Elenna, waving.

"I wanted to come sooner," said Tom, "but there were a few…*problems* to deal with."

His uncle nodded. "Yes, I heard about the dragons."

Tom grinned. His last Quest against Kensa had been one of the deadliest yet. With Vedra and Krimon having done battle in the skies, everyone in Avantia knew about the Beasts now. In a way, Tom was glad the secret was out.

"Wait until the villagers see you," said Henry. "At last you'll get the respect you deserve, *Master* of the Beasts."

Tom blushed. "It's your birthday we're here to celebrate, old man," he said.

Henry narrowed his eyes. "Watch who you call old, little nephew." He flexed his arm. "There's plenty of strength left in these muscles."

Tom laughed. If he knew his uncle, he'd be hammering out axe-heads until he was a toothless eighty-year-old.

"Your aunt's been baking for the last two days," said Henry. "I'll finish up here and join you for a piece of cherry pie."

Tom looked past him, at the blazing hearth. "How about I help you out here?" he said. "Four hands are better than two, and the sooner you're done, the sooner the celebrations can start."

"If you insist," said Uncle Henry, handing him a set of tongs. "I've got a batch of horseshoes to make for old Farmer Jesse."

Tom laid down his knapsack, picked

up a twist of metal and held it in the
fire.

Elenna cleared her throat at the
doorway. "I'll leave you to it," she
said. "I can smell the cherry pie from
here…" Beside her, Silver sniffed
the air and licked his lips. Elenna
laughed. "Looks like Silver can, too."

After Elenna and the wolf had gone,

Tom started to shape the iron with a hammer. It was good to be using his hands for hard work again, and he could feel his uncle's proud gaze.

If I hadn't set off on that journey to the palace, I'd probably be an apprentice blacksmith now, he thought.

"So are you looking forward to the party?" asked Tom.

"Oh yes," said his uncle. "Food, friends, music…"

"Dancing?" said Tom, with a sideways smirk.

Henry groaned. "If I have to!"

CHAPTER FOUR

A TURN FOR THE WORSE

As the sun sank behind the village houses, Tom walked with his aunt, his uncle and Elenna towards the main square. The sound of music drifted in the air, a melody of fiddles and pipes.

"Oh, I almost forgot," said Tom, slipping back into the forge where he'd left his knapsack. He emerged holding the flagon. "Happy birthday, Uncle," he said. "This is King Hugo's finest fruit punch!"

Henry took the flagon, beaming. "What an honour!" he said. "You shouldn't have!"

He tugged out the stopper, brought the flagon to his lips, and took a large swig.

His face screwed up in a grimace.

"Is it all right?" asked Tom.

Uncle Henry swallowed the punch down, looking a little puzzled. "It's... delicious!" he said.

But Tom was sure he'd seen the look of distaste. "You shouldn't drink it if it's gone sour," he said, reaching for the flagon.

His uncle jerked it back and clutched it to his chest, smiling. "Honestly, it's fine." He took another long gulp and some of the purple liquid dribbled down his chin. "See?"

Maybe the punch takes some getting used to, Tom thought, as his uncle took another swig.

When they reached the square, the villagers clapped and cheered. Henry was given a seat at the head of the main table. Tom's stomach rumbled when he saw the food – there was a whole roasted pig, chicken drumsticks and fresh fruit and vegetables of every kind. The village baker, Conrad, had made loaves and twists of honeyed bread dotted with nuts and raisins. The food was simple, but delicious.

When everyone was settled they started to tuck in. Elenna fed scraps of meat to Silver, who was curled up under the bench.

Tom noticed Terrence and some of

his friends on the other side of the
table. They were all staring at him,
but every time Tom looked back, they
lowered their gazes.

"Is everything all right?" he asked.

Terrence blushed. "Is it true…that
you kill huge Beasts?"

Tom shook his head. "We never kill them," he said. "Beasts are good, but Evil magic can make them turn bad. We free Beasts from enchantments, or help return them to their natural homes. Being Master of the Beasts is about keeping the kingdoms in harmony, not killing things."

The children all nodded silently, listening to his every word.

"Tell us about the time you faced the dragon in the mountains," said Terrence. "Is it true he breathes fire?"

Tom grinned. "You mean Ferno," he said. He pulled his shield off his back, and pointed at the black dragon's scale there. "This belonged to him once."

The children gasped.

He told them the story of his very first Beast Quest, to free Ferno from

Malvel's control. By the time he'd finished, he noticed several of the grown-ups were listening as well.

"Tell us another!" said a girl.

"We could be here a long time," Elenna muttered, smiling.

Tom took a bite of cheese, and began the story of his second Quest, to free Sepron the Sea Serpent. He was surprised to realise that, after all this time, he remembered it all so well. The memory of the Beast's rainbow scales, glimmering in the sunlight, still gave him a shiver.

After he'd finished, the children demanded another story. "Maybe Elenna should tell one," said Tom. "After all, she was there, on every single Quest. Without her, I wouldn't be alive today."

It was Elenna's turn to blush, as all

the children switched their gaze to her.

"Sorry to interrupt!" Conrad called from beside Henry. "I think it's time we heard from our birthday boy, don't you?" He gestured towards Tom's uncle. "How about it, Henry? Will you give us a speech?"

The rest of the villagers chanted: "Speech! Speech! Speech!"

Uncle Henry remained seated, looking very uncomfortable.

"Come on, Henry," said Conrad. "Say a few words."

Tom's uncle stood up, frowning. He took another gulp of his punch, then wiped his mouth roughly with the back of his arm. "Thank you all for coming," he said, and sat down heavily.

Silence fell over the table for a

moment, and Tom shared the crowd's disappointment. *He sounds almost ungrateful.* Aunt Maria placed a hand on her husband's arm and whispered in his ear. Uncle Henry jerked his arm away and glared at his plate. He hadn't touched any of the food, Tom noticed.

"I'm sure he just doesn't like the fuss," Elenna murmured.

She turned to address the children, telling them the story of Epos the Flame Bird, bursting from the lava of Stonewin volcano.

"Was it *really* hot?" asked Terrence.

"Hotter than any forge!" said Elenna.

A raised voice came from the head of the table: Uncle Henry's. "Will you leave me alone, woman!" he snapped.

Tom jerked his head to see. His

uncle was on his feet, his face flushed with anger. Aunt Maria looked alarmed.

"I just think you should eat something," she said, reaching for him.

Henry barged past her and picked up a whole cherry pie. "What? Like this soggy mush?" he shouted. "I'd rather go hungry!"

He hurled the pie across the square and it splatted on the ground. Gasps went around the table, and Aunt Maria looked hurt.

Tom stood up, and walked towards them. *Something's not right at all. Maybe he's ill?*

Conrad got there first, positioning himself between Henry and Maria.

"Perhaps you've had enough punch," he said gravely. "Go home and get some rest."

Henry's hand lashed out quickly and raked Conrad's face. "Mind your own business, baker!" he snarled.

For a moment, Conrad clutched his face in shock. When he lowered his hand, deep scratches on his cheek were revealed.

Henry turned on Tom. "And what do *you* want?" he snapped.

Tom took a step back. Something was wrong with his uncle's eyes. Normally they were bright blue, but now they seemed a sickly pale colour, almost yellow. His uncle blinked, and they returned to normal.

I must have imagined it, Tom thought.

He placed a firm hand on his uncle's arm. Henry tried to pull free, but Tom harnessed the magical power of the Golden Breastplate. Extra strength flowed through his muscles, and Henry had no chance of escaping.

"Conrad's right," Tom said. "You should go home."

The look of anger on Henry's face cleared for a moment, and he nodded. Tom felt his arm relax. He released his uncle, and watched him stagger off towards home.

Elenna came to Tom's side. "I never knew Henry had such a temper," she said.

"He doesn't normally," muttered Tom, watching his uncle leave.

Aunt Maria was shaking her head. "I'm so sorry, everyone," she said.

Conrad put an arm round her. "Never mind. Henry's been guzzling that punch all night," he said. "It must have gone to his head."

The party was over, and the villagers began to make their way home.

"Let's get some sleep," said Elenna. "I'm sure things will seem better in the morning."

Tom accompanied his aunt on the way back. He wished he could agree with Elenna, but he was thinking of the warnings Daltec had given them as they left the City.

Perhaps he was right to be afraid…

CHAPTER FIVE

A DEADLY TRAIL

Tom woke to the sound of screaming, and then a crash.

What's happening?

He sprang out of bed, grabbed his sword and shield in the darkness, and ran out of the room. His uncle and aunt's bedroom was opposite, and the door was open.

Inside, Maria was in her nightdress, crouched in a corner, hugging her

knees. Tears were running down her
cheeks. Tom looked around for his
uncle, but he wasn't there. A dresser
had fallen on its side, and a broken
vase lay in shards on the floor.

"He's gone mad!" said Maria.
"Please, Tom, find him!"

Elenna came into the room,
carrying a candle. "I heard

shouting…" she said.

"Henry's gone," said Tom. He noticed then that there were patches of water on the floor – wet footprints leading out of the room. *That's odd…*

Tom helped his aunt to her feet, and sat her on the bed. He couldn't see any injuries, but her eyes shone with fear.

"What happened?" he said.

She shook her head, as if trying to avoid a thought. "I woke up and he was standing by the window, looking out," she said. "His whole body was shaking. I asked what was wrong, but he didn't seem to hear me… Then he opened his eyes…" Maria put a hand to her mouth. "And his eyes weren't his! He pushed me, and I fell. Then he just shot across the room, knocking the dresser over."

"We'll find him," Tom said to his aunt. "Just stay here where it's safe."

Elenna had found her bow and quiver and slung them over her shoulder. They followed the footprints through the house together.

Tom couldn't work out why they were wet. *Perhaps Henry spilled some water…*

The front door hung off its hinges, as if it had been kicked open. Beside it, Tom saw King Hugo's flagon and picked it up. He sniffed the neck and almost gagged. The dregs of the punch smelled bitter and rotten, nothing like the delicious aroma he had smelled back at the palace.

"What's got into him?" said Tom. "Is it the punch?"

Elenna smelled the flagon too, and made a face. "It could be. I don't know, though."

Tom felt a guilty ache in his stomach. *I brought the punch to Errinel,* he thought. *This is my fault!*

They stepped outside into the night air. "Henry!" called Tom. "Uncle, where are you?"

There was no reply. Tom followed the footprints across the deserted square, past the empty tables. The prints were spaced far apart, as if Henry was running. *If he's ill, he might hurt himself,* Tom thought. *The sooner we bring him home, the better.*

As they tracked the wet marks, Tom's worry turned to panic. The prints led right out of the village, past the houses, towards the marshes south of Errinel. As a young boy, he and his friends had never been allowed this way, because it was dangerous. The grown-ups said that sheep and cows sometimes strayed into the marshes and sank in the mud, becoming trapped. A fog hung over the dank waters most days, and it was easy to get lost and find yourself in trouble. Tom could see the fog now, like a grey blanket smothering the horizon.

"There!" said Elenna.

She pointed out a shape in the gloom. Some sort of figure, carrying a gleaming shield on its back, was heading in the direction of the marshes.

My uncle! thought Tom. He darted after the figure, Elenna close behind.

"Henry," he cried. "Come back!"

They ran through a line of trees, and when they emerged on the other side, Tom's breath caught in his chest. A shaft of moonlight lit up the figure

– it wasn't his uncle at all. It was too big to be a man. And what he had thought was a shield was something completely different.

"It's a shell," Tom realised. "It's a Beast with a shell, like a turtle. We need to stop it before it finds my uncle."

"I don't like this," said Elenna. The sudden sound of hooves interrupted her, and Tom turned to see Storm galloping towards them, eyes wild. "He must have escaped from the stables," Elenna said. Silver followed, growling at the shape up ahead.

He must have tracked our scent, Tom thought. He turned back towards the marshes and saw the shelled figure disappearing into the mists. They rushed after it, their panting breaths becoming steaming clouds in the cold air.

The ground became muddy as they neared the marshes, gripping at the soles of Tom's boots with a sucking sound. He held up a hand to Storm. "Stay here!" he said. He couldn't risk the stallion sinking and becoming trapped.

Ahead, the footprints on the ground changed. Instead of five toes, Tom could see only three wide ones, which seemed to be webbed. They were much larger too. It made him think of a toad. A giant one.

"I don't understand," said Tom. "It's like the creature is changing. What are we chasing here? And where's Henry?"

Wisps of mist drifted over the marshes like pale ghosts. "Your uncle must have gone in there with the Beast," whispered Elenna. "But why?"

Tom's chest felt tight with fear, but he strode forward into the marshes, with Elenna and Silver at his heels. They jumped between black pools of stagnant water in the soggy ground, which sank slightly at each step.

As he moved, Tom thought back to Henry's eyes flashing yellow – right after he'd been drinking the sour-smelling punch. But the flagon had been with Tom the whole time – from when the palace servant gave it to him, to when he passed it on to his uncle.

Not quite, he realised. *There was the short while when I was looking for bandits on the road, when the old woman came.*

A terrible chill spread through his chest as he remembered the mysterious old woman...the flagon lying on its side, the stopper loose...

"Tom?" said Elenna. "You've gone pale."

Tom stared at his friend, a horrible thought forming in his mind. *My uncle vanished, and this Beast appeared. What if they're the same thing? What if the Beast is my uncle?*

"I have a nasty feeling," he said in a whisper, "that Uncle Henry is in terrible danger."

CHAPTER SIX

PLAGUE OF THE DAMNED

Silver let out a snarl behind them, and Tom turned. Back by the trees, he saw a familiar shape emerge. It was Conrad, the baker. Aunt Maria's scream must have woken him too.

"This way!" called Tom. "Henry's gone into the marshes."

Conrad stumbled drunkenly out of the trees, coming towards them.

"Is he all right?" asked Elenna.

Silver leaped in front of Tom and Elenna, baring his teeth and growling at the approaching villager. Elenna gripped the fur of his neck and hauled him back.

"Conrad?" said Tom. The baker was almost running at them now, snatching at the air with claw-like hands. His eyes flashed the same sickly yellow as Henry's had the evening before. Drool spilled from Conrad's slack lips, and a foul smell drifted from his body. *The same smell that came from the empty flask of punch*, Tom thought. *But Conrad didn't drink any...*

Tom's hand found the hilt of his sword. "Conrad, stop!" he shouted.

The baker threw himself at Tom, reaching for his throat. Tom ducked

out of the way as Conrad stumbled
past. He drew his blade, just to scare
the villager off. Silver snapped his
jaws, but Elenna held him tightly.

As Conrad turned his yellow eyes on
them, Tom saw the scratches on his
cheek where Henry had struck him.
They were oozing green pus. *That's
where the terrible smell is coming from*,
Tom thought. *He's infected with the same*

poison as my uncle! It must have passed over when he was scratched.

Conrad came at him again. With no choice, Tom swung the flat of his blade against Conrad's legs. The baker folded with a groan.

"Tom, look out!" cried Elenna.

Tom felt a vice-like grip on his sword arm, and found himself face to face with another villager – Karen the seamstress, an old friend of Maria. When he was a boy getting into scrapes and climbing trees, Karen had always mended his clothes. But there was no kindness in her face now. Her yellow eyes bored into him, as if hungry for his flesh. He caught a glimpse of something on her neck. *Are those...tooth-marks?* Tom pushed her away from him and fell backwards – straight into another set of arms.

It was Mikkel, a young farmer who tended crops and raised sheep in Errinel.

Tom writhed, but Mikkel pulled him closer, his mouth gaping as he lowered his teeth to Tom's shoulder.

"No!" cried Elenna.

From the corner of his eye, Tom saw her bow swing round and crack Mikkel over the back of his head. His eyes rolled back and he crumpled at Tom's feet, unconscious.

Tom and Elenna backed away from the villagers. Conrad and Karen were on their feet already and Mikkel was stirring. Silver snapped and snarled at them, but seemed unwilling to attack.

He doesn't want to catch the infection, Tom thought.

"What's going on, Tom?" said Elenna. She brandished her bow like a staff, stabbing and swinging as the villagers lumbered towards them.

"It's the punch!" said Tom. "It must have contained some sort of poison that turned Uncle Henry into that shelled Beast. Then when my uncle scratched Conrad, he must have passed the infection on. It's some sort of plague!"

The whole village might be affected, for

all we know!

Elenna jabbed Conrad in the chest and knocked him back. But Mikkel seized the end of her bow. Elenna twisted it and tugged it free. "We have to get word to Daltec," she said. "This is some sort of enchantment."

Tom used his shield to push Karen away.

"Just don't get scratched or bitten,"

he said to Elenna. "We might be all that stands between this plague and the whole kingdom!"

Suddenly, the glow of fire lit up the hideous faces of the Infected.

"Get away!" said a voice.

Tom turned and saw villagers pouring towards them, all carrying flaming torches or simple weapons like knives and clubs. They walked upright, rather than hunched and lumbering.

They're not infected after all!

At the sight of the armed band, Mikkel, Karen and Conrad turned and fled towards the marshes, grunting and shrieking as they staggered away.

"It was the fire," said Elenna. "I think that's what scared them off."

Tom sucked in a deep breath, and

sheathed his sword. He checked his arms for scratches, relieved not to find any.

The villagers reached them, led by Ned the butcher, and his two sons Gavyn and Rob.

"Maria told us what happened," said Ned. "We came to help you find Henry. What were those things?"

"They were villagers," said Tom. "Some Evil spell has changed them."

"A spell?" said Ned.

Tom glanced in the direction of the marshes, where the mist seemed to be thickening by the second. "I think so. I don't know the full story yet, but while there's blood in my veins I'll get to the bottom of this."

"We'll come with you," said Ned.

Tom shook his head. He couldn't let the villagers go into those mists until

he knew what awaited them. Either
they would get themselves infected
too, or worse, they might kill Henry
or one of the others.

"Elenna and I will go after them,"
Tom told the villagers. "You stay here,
and look after Storm."

"You can't face that danger alone," Rob said.

Tom gave a grim smile. "This is what we're good at. Leave it to us."

CHAPTER SEVEN

OKAWA

Tom and Elenna took a torch each
from the villagers and hurried
towards the marshes, with Silver
keeping pace at their side. Tom
looked back as the mist enveloped
them, pleased to see that Ned and
his band had obeyed his instructions.
Gavyn was standing with a hand
on Storm's neck, and the stallion
twitched nervously.

Tom held his torch close to the ground, following the webbed footprints. "I've been thinking about that old woman on the road," he said. "When I went to look for the bandits, there was no sign of them or any struggle. I think she was lying…"

Elenna gasped. "She must have been distracting us so she could do something to the punch!"

Silver had trotted on ahead, nose to the ground. His paws left imprints in the soft mud. Tufts of grass grew here and there.

The night was silent apart from their breathing and the soft shush of water flowing somewhere ahead. "There's a river here," said Tom. "Be careful, some of this marsh is treacherous."

"I remember," said Elenna. "This

is near where we battled Soltra the Stone Charmer."

Tom shuddered. Fighting the Beast of the marshes had almost cost them their lives.

Tom held his sword aloft, and his shield was ready on his arm. The fog shifted across their path, like shadows rushing through the darkness. Even though they were out in the open, he felt trapped. The mists parted in front of them and closed behind. His eyes strained, trying to pick out any movement. His mouth was dry.

"Henry!" he called out. The mists seemed to swallow his cry. Even if his uncle could hear him, Tom suspected he wouldn't come. *Whatever was in that punch changed him.*

A gust of wind blew across from the east, snatching at the fog. For a moment, the way ahead cleared, and Tom saw the river flowing across their path twenty paces away. The water was black and shining.

"What's that?" said Elenna, pointing to their left. Tom looked, but the mists had closed in again.

"I think I saw someone," Elenna said. "By the riverbank."

Tom tried to calm his breathing, but his pulse was racing as they headed off again. Their torches turned the grey mist the same strange dull yellow as he'd seen in the eyes of the Infected. Then the hairs on his neck prickled, and he sensed something approaching from behind them. He turned, and saw a large shape coming at them through the gloom.

Storm nosed through the fog with a whinny, head bowed, and Tom breathed a sigh of relief.

"He must have broken free," said
Elenna. "He didn't want to wait
behind."

Tom ran a hand down Storm's
nose, and the warmth coming from
the stallion's body was a comfort.

The ground was firmer here and the webbed prints were harder to make out. But at least Storm wouldn't get bogged down. It felt good to have the stallion at his side.

The four of them crept on. Tom guessed they were almost at the river bank.

Then, with an eerie howl, another gust blew through. The mists lifted and he gasped.

Right at the water's edge, a person was crouching, shrouded in mist.

No, not a person, Tom thought, dread tugging at his heart. *It's too big to be a human. Something else.*

He held his torch out, and saw that the thing had legs, long and slimy and covered in green scales like a reptile. It seemed to be dipping its head into the water; not drinking, but dunking it right under the surface.

"What *are* you?" Tom whispered.

As the Beast half straightened,
Tom saw its shell. Long and curved,
covering the creature's back, it looked
like green, roughly plated armour.

It turned slowly towards them,
rising to a height that was twice as tall
as a normal man. Its face was narrow,

with scaled blue-green skin stretched
tight over pinched features. Its mouth
had no lips and its nose was flat. As
far as Tom could see, it had no ears at
all. Black slashes in its neck gaped like
a fish's gills.

The creature took a step towards
them on webbed feet, and clawed
arms, sinewy with muscle, hung at its
sides.

But the strangest thing was its
forehead. The skull looked hollowed
out at the top, filled with water that
sloshed over the edges. Tom had
never seen anything like it.

Storm snorted, stamping his hooves.

The Beast made no move to attack
them, but stared intently through
slitted yellow eyes with black pupils,
just like a snake's. As Tom stared
back, he felt a mixture of horror and

fear and something else – sympathy.

He didn't need the ruby jewel of Torgor to tell him the dreadful truth about the creature before him. Despite its hideous appearance he recognised something familiar in the face. Tom's fears were right. This was his uncle, changed by some terrible magic.

"Henry?" he said.

The creature's mouth split into a smile of pure evil.

"No," it hissed, and its forked black tongue darted out like an eel. "I am not your uncle any longer. My name is Okawa, and you have made me what I am!"

STORY TWO

My fears have been realised.

The forces of Good in the kingdom must remain vigilant at all times, for Evil never rests. The dark visions I see in Tom's home village are proof of this. But Tom will meet them head on – the kingdom's greatest protector will face down any threat, especially a threat to his beloved family.

I must go to him at once. Now that Evil has targeted his family in the worst possible way, I fear the Master of the Beasts might let his anger cloud his judgement. If that happens, he could make a costly mistake...

He needs my help.

Daltec,
Wizard of Avantia

CHAPTER ONE

DROWNED

Tom stared in horror at the Beast.
Could it really be true? Was this thing
all that remained of the man who had
raised him?

Okawa lunged towards them, his
webbed feet slapping in the mud.

I can't hurt my own uncle, thought
Tom, looking at his sword.

"Run!" he yelled, backing away and
pulling Elenna with him. "And stay

clear of his claws."

If Okawa infects us too, the kingdom will be at Kensa's mercy.

Tom smacked Storm's flank and the stallion galloped away, Tom and Elenna following his path. They fled across the marsh back towards the trees. Tom wasn't watching where he put his boots, and several times they sank into wet ground, soaking his feet. He heard Elenna's heavy breathing behind him, and looked back. She was only a few paces behind, reaching as she ran for an arrow in her quiver. He couldn't see Okawa, but he could hear grunting and pounding footsteps. Then the mists parted for a moment and he saw the Beast. His huge, slippery body seemed to glide across the marsh, his webbed feet hardly breaking the

surface of the boggy ground. All the
while he kept his head level, barely
spilling a drop of the water from the
strange cup in his skull.

The mist thickened around them again, and Tom lost his bearings. Where were the trees? Surely they'd come far enough. If he didn't know better, he'd think that Okawa was controlling the fog, using it to trap them.

He saw the river's edge, ahead and to the left. "We're running in a circle," he said to Elenna. "This way!"

He ran away from the water, spotting the spidery branches of the tree line. Another bank of mist rolled in, making his tunic damp. He couldn't see more than three paces ahead.

CRACK!

Something hit his head and Tom fell back onto the wet ground, dazed. He reached up to touch his head and brought away a bloodied hand.

"What…?" he mumbled, his eyes blurring.

"Tom?" he heard Elenna cry. "Where did you go?"

As his vision cleared, he saw a low branch above him. *I must have run into it…*

A vice-like grip fastened on his ankle, yanking him through the slimy mud.

"Elenna!" he cried.

He looked over his shoulder and saw Okawa holding his foot with a clawed hand. The Beast was pulling him along with just one muscular arm. Fear blossomed in his chest.

He's so strong, Tom thought.

He tried to tug his leg free, but Okawa only jerked harder. Tom drew his sword and drove it into the ground, trying to slow his progress.

He clung to the hilt with all his might, but felt his mud-coated fingers slipping. Through the red jewel, he heard Okawa's voice.

You're coming with me, Avantian. I'll hold you under the depths until water fills your lungs.

"No you won't," said Tom, gritting his teeth. He wriggled his foot, sliding it free of his boot. Okawa staggered backwards holding the empty boot, then tossed it aside. His eyes glowed with hatred.

A grey shape leaped over the top of Tom and hit Okawa, paws-first, in the middle of his chest.

Silver!

Okawa cried out and staggered backwards. Tom scrambled forward to collect his boot. As he struggled to get it back on, he saw that Silver had now dropped to the ground with a snarl, before launching himself again. With a vicious backwards swipe of his hand, Okawa struck the wolf and sent him sliding across the ground with a pitiful whine. Silver plunged into a muddy pool beside the river and lay still.

"No!" screamed Elenna.

She ran past Tom, tossing aside her bow as she threw herself to her knees at the wolf's side. Silver was sinking, his muzzle already beneath the water. Elenna plunged her hands in, trying to rescue him from the sucking pool.

Okawa strode towards Tom, claws shining in the dim moonlight. *I've got no choice*, Tom thought, lifting his sword ready to defend himself. But at the last moment, the Beast turned. His slitted eyes settled on Elenna, still with her back to him, cradling Silver's head. Okawa started to walk towards her.

"Elenna! Look out!" Tom yelled.

Elenna managed to heave Silver onto the bank and turned, reaching for her bow. Tom caught the flash of fear in her eyes as she realised it

wasn't there. He began to run over, but his boots were waterlogged and heavy. *I'm too slow!*

Okawa leaped at his friend, pulling her into the river with a huge splash. The last thing Tom saw was the Beast's glinting shell sinking beneath the surface, taking Elenna with him.

CHAPTER TWO

TUG-OF-WAR

Tom waded into the water, sword held high. His eyes darted left and right in panic, looking for some sign of his friend. He couldn't let her die like this, drowned in the filthy marsh water.

Tom walked further out, until the water reached his chest. It was black as oil – he couldn't see a thing beneath the surface.

"Elenna!" he cried.

His clothes and skin were clogged with thick mud. It took all the strength of his Golden Breastplate just to hold his sword out of the water.

"Elenna!" he repeated.

The water exploded to his left and Elenna's head and neck emerged. Her mouth gaped to suck in a huge breath, then clawed hands gripped her shoulders and pulled her back under. Okawa's shell rolled through the water and sank too. Legs and arms thrashed and churned as the two fought in the water.

Elenna's putting up a fight!

Tom waded nearer, feeling the uneven ground shift and cling to his feet. He saw the tip of the Beast's shell break the surface and slammed the hilt of his sword onto it. The Beast

roared and spun, lashing out a clawed
hand which wrapped around Tom's
throat.

With a growl, Okawa hurled him
across the water. Tom crashed onto
the muddy bank, the air knocked

from his lungs. He pushed wet hair from his face, gasping. Silver was up and pacing the bank, howling desperately as the Beast plunged Elenna under again.

What can I do? Okawa's too strong!

Tom's eyes fell on Elenna's bow, half submerged in the mud. He sheathed his sword and picked up the bow, turning the curved wood in his hands. Silver suddenly stopped

howling and snatched something up in his jaws from the river's edge. A single arrow.

It must have fallen out of her quiver when the Beast dragged her in.

Silver let the arrow drop at Tom's feet.

I don't have Elenna's skill, Tom wanted to say.

Looking out to the water, he saw Okawa standing tall, his arms beneath the water. Elenna had stopped thrashing. *She doesn't have much longer!*

Tom set the shaft to the bow, and stretched back the string. *That's Uncle Henry out there*, he thought desperately, *but I've got no choice. Elenna will die!*

His muscles were aching from the earlier fight, and his arms trembled as he pulled the bowstring back. He aimed at the Beast's shell. Perhaps it would be enough to distract him rather than kill him…

If Tom could hit his target.

He had one arrow – one shot to save Elenna's life.

Her voice crept into his head as he remembered the times she'd tried to teach him.

Steady yourself from your feet to your head. Most archers miss because they are twitching when they fire.

Tom planted his feet apart, and forced his arms to go still.

Bring your eye level with the arrow. Look at the target, not the arrowhead.

Tom stared along the shaft, focusing on Okawa's shell.

Take a deep breath in.

Tom drew air into his nose, and felt his pounding heart grow calm.

Then breathe out, release, and let the arrow do the rest.

Tom fired, and the arrow sang through the air, burying itself between two plates in Okawa's shell.

With a shrill shriek, Okawa staggered back, releasing Elenna. He

thrashed and growled in the water, and fear hit Tom in the gut. *What if I've just mortally wounded Uncle Henry?*

Elenna surfaced and began to swim weakly towards the shore as the Beast reached his long arms over his shoulders and gripped the arrow shaft. With a hiss, he snapped the shaft off near the point and glared at it. His gaze shifted to Tom on the shore, his voice filling Tom's head.

It'll take more than that to stop me.

He sank beneath the water, out of sight.

Tom ran into the marsh shallows as Elenna neared the bank. He reached out his arm to pull her to safety. As her fingers closed around his, her mouth suddenly went wide and she lurched back into the water. "Help me!" she cried.

Okawa rose up behind her, his hands clutching her ankles. He gave a hideous grin, and a long black tongue darted over his lipless face like a wriggling eel.

"Don't let me go!" Elenna pleaded.

Tom dug his heels into the soft ground and heaved for all he was worth, drawing on the power of the Golden Breastplate once again. He managed to drag her a few feet towards the bank, but Okawa hauled her back in again. *He's too strong! I need another plan.*

Silver was snarling and snapping on the bank, but Okawa barely seemed to notice.

Tom knew what he had to do, but he dreaded to think how it might harm his uncle.

He gathered his strength, and all

the power of the Golden Breastplate.
It might not be enough to get Elenna
ashore, but it would give Tom the
few seconds he needed. With a grunt,
he heaved on Elenna's arms. She
let out a yell of pain, and Okawa
stumbled forward. As the Beast found
his footing, Tom let go of Elenna
with his right hand, drew his sword,
and slashed the blade at the Beast's
outstretched arm. The steel bit deep
into Okawa's green flesh, and dark
blood spurted from the wound.

With a deafening screech, the Beast toppled backwards, releasing his hold and disappearing into the marsh.

Elenna scrambled to safety, and fell to her knees beside Silver. Tom sank onto the muddy bank at her side.

"Are you all right?" he panted.

"I think so," she replied. Silver was licking her face.

Then Tom saw her leg and despair ran through his heart like a shard of ice. It was bleeding, just above the knee.

"Elenna," he said, pointing to the wound, "please tell me that's a nick from my sword, and not..."

Elenna looked terrified. She shook her head, as though she was afraid to believe the sight in front of her eyes. If it wasn't Tom's blade which had wounded her, it must have

been Okawa's claws. She pulled
back the torn trousers and Tom saw
two scratch marks, just like those
on Conrad's cheek. "No…" she
mumbled. "Please…not that…"

"It'll be all right," said Tom, but
even as he spoke the words, he knew
they were empty. *It won't be all right.
She'll turn, just like the others…*

Silver growled and they both looked up. Okawa's head rose above the water a few paces out and Tom heard the Beast's voice in his head, every word dripping with triumph.

She's mine now.

CHAPTER THREE

A SECRET CHANNEL

The Beast gave a rasping laugh, and Tom wished he couldn't hear its voice in his head.

Your friend is as good as dead, said Okawa. *She will be my slave soon!*

Elenna doubled over, grimacing. "I'm...changing," she said. "I can feel it happening. Tom, help me!"

Silver whined softly, sniffing, and

took a step back.

Her scent's confusing him, Tom thought. *He can smell the poison inside her.*

Tom helped Elenna to her feet, then turned to Okawa. Maybe he could free his friend, by defeating the source of the evil – the Beast himself. It was his only hope.

Okawa must have sensed his plan, because he backed off.

You'll have to catch me first, said the Beast's voice. Then it spun and swam away. Tom jumped into the water after him, ignoring Elenna's cries of "Stop! Don't!"

He chased the shell of Okawa, but the Beast dipped beneath the surface and was gone. Tom took a breath and dived, but it was hopeless – he couldn't see a thing in the dank water. But if he didn't catch Okawa, Elenna had no chance. He felt about blindly, then came up for air. The surface was calm. The Beast was nowhere to be seen.

Tom waded back towards the shore, where Silver was guarding Elenna at a distance. Storm had returned to their side, and was now standing anxiously over Tom's friend, who lay on her back, her eyes staring miserably at the sky.

I've failed, he thought. *First Uncle Henry, now Elenna. The Quest is over.*

"Don't give up hope," said a voice. "All is not lost."

Tom turned with a gasp. A figure hovered just above the water.

"Daltec!"

The Wizard's shimmering image floated closer. "Okawa has slipped

through your clutches. Now it's a race
against time."

"Elenna's been infected!" said Tom.

"More than Elenna is at stake," said
Daltec. "Okawa is on his way to the
City!"

"The City?" said Elenna weakly.
"But how?"

Daltec pointed out across the water.

"There are underwater caves on the other side of the river, and a tunnel that leads all the way to Avantia's capital. It's the quickest route to the City by far."

"If Okawa reaches the City," said Tom, "he'll infect *everyone*!"

Daltec nodded. "That can't be allowed to happen. You'll have to follow him, Tom."

"And I'll come with you," Elenna began. As she tried to sit up, she sank back with a moan of pain.

"You cannot join this fight, Elenna," said Daltec. "I'll magic you back to the palace and begin work on an antidote to cure the poison."

He muttered some words under his breath. In a flash of light, Elenna, Silver and Storm disappeared.

"Are you staying with me?" asked

Tom. "I could use some magical help."

"I wish I could," said Daltec, "but if I don't start on an antidote for Elenna, it will be too late for her. Even a Wizard can't be in two places at once. You have to stop Okawa in the tunnel, Tom. If you do not, all the Infected will have to be treated as enemies of Avantia."

Tom had never seen the young Wizard's face so grave. As the words sank in, their meaning became clear.

"But Elenna…Conrad…all the innocent villagers. Uncle Henry!"

"They belong to Okawa now," said Daltec. "Stop him, Tom. It's the only way."

Daltec reached into his robes and drew out a lit candle. The flame burned, straight up, not even flickering in the breeze, and Tom realised it was magical. He took it, hope filling his heart.

"This will help light your way," said Daltec. "The candle burns even beneath the water. Good luck, Tom."

With those words, Daltec vanished.

While there's blood in my veins, thought Tom, *I will not fail.*

He slipped into the water and swam out with powerful strokes towards the spot where Daltec had pointed, staying alert. He knew that Okawa could be waiting for him in the darkness.

Scrabbling at the river bank, Tom found the cave's rocky opening – half submerged. He swam through.

Stalactites like stone daggers hung from the roof, but Tom couldn't see any tunnel. *It must be underwater*, he realised. He took a deep breath, and dived. Sure enough the candle's flame didn't die underwater – it burned on, throwing an eerie glow ahead. At any moment, Tom expected to see Okawa lunge from the shadows with his raking claws, but no attack came.

At the far end of the cave, Tom found a hole under the waterline, a black mouth leading into the

unknown. He raised his head above the water, taking another deep breath before submerging again. He swam into the underwater tunnel. Fine dust floated in the current, and mosses grew from the rocky walls. Already his breath was running out. *If only I had the Pearl of Gwildor to help me breathe beneath the water…*

He swam on – it was too far to go back now. His lungs began to burn.

Tom desperately clawed his way along the tunnel as the current carried him onward, looking for any sign of a way out.

Fear set in, making his heart beat even faster. *I need to stay calm – I'll only use up more breath if I start to panic.*

But still he saw no sign of the tunnel's end. He imagined his lifeless body floating down there for years. Just a skeleton bobbing along in the dark water.

No one would ever find him.

No one would ever come looking.

Perhaps this was all a terrible mistake…

Above Tom, the rock suddenly gave way to open water. He kicked hard, swimming upwards, trying not to think of his aching lungs.

Tom's head burst through the water and he sucked down huge breaths of stale, cold air. He was in some sort of pool at the edge of an underground cavern. Dragging his sodden body out of the water, he kneeled on the muddy bank, waiting until he felt strong enough to stand.

Glancing around, he saw footprints. Webbed footprints. They led away into the darkness.

I've found your trail, Okawa, Tom thought.

He clambered to his feet and followed the tracks onwards through another tunnel, breaking into a run.

You won't get away from me!

CHAPTER FOUR

CITY IN PERIL

The tunnel was straight, but felt to
Tom like it was endless. From the
wide spacing of Okawa's footprints,
Tom guessed the Beast was running
too. Though his own legs ached, he
didn't let up. He was racing to save the
whole kingdom. Underground, with
no sight of the sky, it was hard to tell
how much time had passed, how far
he'd run, or even whether it was night

or day. The only sounds were the dripping walls, the slap of his feet and the ragged breathing in his throat.

Tom's mind blanked out, focusing on running alone. *The kingdom needs me.* His eyes scanned the darkness ahead for the Beast's shape, but he never saw even a glimpse of the gleaming shell. *Okawa's probably reached the City already.*

Tom's fears came true. The tunnel began to slope upwards and he heard screams and shouts of panic. *I'm too late! Okawa's arrived.* Tom followed the sounds, drawing his sword. A faint light seeped into the passage, and he tossed the magical candle aside.

At last he reached an iron grille, which had been prised open. Okawa had definitely come this way – slime dripped from the metal.

Tom pushed it aside and climbed out.

He saw at once that he was just inside
the City walls, at the end of a drainage
ditch. He'd walked past it a hundred
times, but never realised where it
went. From the position of the sun
in the sky, he guessed it was around
noon. He realised he must have been
running all night, and sudden fatigue

made his vision swim. Tom steadied himself against the wall. *Must…keep…going.*

He climbed onto the City's wall and jogged towards one of the main streets, the screams and cries below growing more intense. He skidded to a halt. Three people, their eyes yellow with madness, were clawing at the door of a house and pounding it with their fists. Despair filled Tom's heart. How many had been infected already?

He could hear shouts coming from inside the house as the Infected launched themselves at the timbers. *It won't be long before they break through…*

Tom saw a cart laden with barrels nearby. It gave him an idea. *A distraction.*

He placed his fingers in his mouth and let out a shrill whistle. The plagued Avantians all turned their yellow gazes on him. Tom jumped down into the street and quickly unhooked the back of the cart. The barrels bounced off, flying at the Infected. They screeched and leaped away from the door to dodge the barrels. Then they spotted Tom, and ran at him, their arms outstretched. Tom sprinted in the opposite direction,

leading them away from the house.

Tom reached the main City gates.
There he found a line of soldiers, all
gripping spears. Captain Harkman
stood above them on the walls.

"Stay in formation!" the captain
bellowed. "Keep them back!"

A crowd of Infected faced the
soldiers, their faces twisted in savage
hunger. Tom saw a kitchen boy he
knew, his eyes yellow and sickly.
There was a soldier too, with scratches
down his cheek.

"Tom," shouted Captain Harkman,
"the City's gone mad!"

"There's a Beast on the loose," Tom
said. "It passes infection through
scratches. Try and get the uninfected
to safety."

Captain Harkman nodded, wide-
eyed. "And what are you going to

do?" he asked.

"I'm going to track it down," said Tom, and he set off running towards the Palace. *I just hope Daltec's finished the antidote by now.*

He was a few paces away when a crowd of Infected blocked his path. They gnashed their teeth, spitting yellow foam and raking their clawed hands towards him.

I have to get past. But I mustn't get scratched!

Tom ducked beneath a swiping hand, then shouldered the infected man out of the way. Another jumped at him – a little girl – but he raised his shield, and she toppled over his head. As she landed, she sprang back up again. Tom didn't fancy waiting around. He placed his foot on a water trough and leaped over the heads of

the Infected, then dashed through a door, slamming it closed behind him. The wood shuddered as the Infected threw themselves at it from the other side. He could hear their snarls and grunts.

Tom dropped the wooden bar over

the hooks to secure the door and ran up the stairs towards Daltec's chamber. He burst in, and skidded to a halt at the sight before him.

Elenna lay on the bed, her wrists and ankles tied to the posts. Her face was feverish and sweaty, but her eyes were closed. Daltec kneeled beside her, dabbing at her forehead with a damp cloth.

"Elenna?" Tom said.

"She's fought the infection far longer than most," said Daltec, "but it's taking her over."

I let her down, thought Tom, his heart heavy. *I should have saved her.*

"Have you had any luck with a cure?" he asked.

The Wizard shook his head, and gestured at the desk and floor, littered with open books. "I've searched my shelves here, and found nothing. But there may be something in the library."

Tom glanced at his friend again. Her chest rose and fell with shallow breaths.

"Then we'd better get there quickly. But we'll have to be careful – half the city seems to be infected."

He went to the door, listening for any sound outside.

"Not that way," said Daltec. He walked towards the large fireplace. "I know a safer route." Frowning, Tom watched as Daltec stepped into the hearth. "Come on."

Tom followed him, ducking under the mantelpiece. Daltec reached up and grabbed a rope hanging from one side of the brickwork. He yanked it. The ashy ground beneath Tom's feet shifted with a grinding sound, and they began to descend.

"I never knew this was here," said Tom as the darkness swallowed them.

Daltec's voice was weary. "A Wizard always has secrets."

It was hard to tell how fast or how far they went down, but after a few moments, the contraption stopped in front of a bookcase. "Here we are," said Daltec, pushing the shelves open like a door. They were standing at the back of the library.

Daltec headed straight to a shelf labelled *Magic and Spells*. "Better get searching," he said.

Tom scanned the spines of the books, looking for anything about enchantments and evil magic. He saw titles about summoning ghosts, levitation, invisibility…

The sound of soft footsteps made him spin around, ears straining.

"What was that?" he whispered. Had some Infected somehow entered the library? He drew his sword, and edged around the bookcase. A shadow slipped across the aisle ahead. Tom crept out.

He heard the steps again, just around the next bookcase.

Daltec arrived at his side, face pale.

Tom held up his hand, to say *Stay back!*

Then he leaped into the open, sword raised. A figure sat hunched over a table. "Don't move!" Tom shouted.

"Is that how you welcome an old friend?" The voice was familiar...

"Petra!" said Tom.

The young witch turned to face him with a lopsided smile. Tom's grip

on his sword tightened – with Petra,
he never knew if he was talking to a
friend or a foe. She had been both on
many occasions.

"That's right." She peered past him.
"And if it isn't Aduro's apprentice,
young Daltec. I hope your spells are
improving, because you'll need some
powerful magic to stop this plague."

"What are you doing here?" asked Tom.

Petra held up a book she'd been reading. "The same thing as you – I'm looking for a cure. You're just in time to congratulate me for finding it."

Daltec came forward and snatched up the book, his eyes moving quickly over the text. "She's right," he said. "The poison is called 'Riverturn'."

Petra smiled smugly. "See? I remember Malvel telling me once how to make the potion."

"It must have been in King Hugo's fruit punch," said Tom.

"But why isn't the King infected?" Daltec asked.

Tom ran a hand through his hair anxiously. "The poison wasn't put in the flagon until after I'd left the City," he said. "We met an old woman on the road. She distracted Elenna and me. She must have slipped something in the flagon."

"What old woman?" asked Daltec.

Tom kicked at the table leg as the final piece of the puzzle fell into place. *I never actually saw the old woman's face properly.*

"I've been so stupid… I knew Kensa would strike again!"

"Kensa is behind this?" said Petra.

"She was right under my nose," said Tom bitterly. "She must have thought that I would drink the poison – but instead I gave it to my uncle. I should have figured this out sooner. And now the whole of Avantia will be infected."

CHAPTER FIVE

FACING OKAWA

"This is no time to think about the past," said Daltec. "Right now, we have to cure the Infected." He traced the page with his finger. "There's a recipe for an antidote here. I think all the ingredients are in Aduro's stores, but they'll take a while to gather. It says the mixture 'must be placed in a burning flame, before being taken'."

"Will there be enough to cure

everyone?" asked Tom.

Daltec's lips pressed together and then he spoke again. "It says here that the antidote must be applied to the source of the curse, and then it will be lifted."

"The source – that must be Okawa," Tom said. "You two mix the cure. Meanwhile, I'll keep the Beast busy."

He took the secret route back to Daltec's room. Elenna was on the bed where he'd left her, lying completely still. *Too still*, thought Tom. *Is she even breathing?*

He crouched beside the bed and laid a hand on her arm.

Elenna's eyes snapped open, glowing with yellow hatred. She thrashed in her bonds, spittle flying from her lips as she snapped at him. Tom jumped back, but then stared

down in pity.

My friend is still in there, buried somewhere.

"I promise I'll save you," he said, then rushed out of the door.

Elenna's snarls followed him down the stairs. He hesitated a moment in front of the barred doorway, then

lifted the bar and stepped out. The
crowd of Infected had disappeared,
but cries of fear came from the
courtyard.

He rounded a corner and saw city
folk scattering as Okawa rampaged.
Soldiers tried to block the way with
their shields, but Okawa swatted
them aside with his powerful arms.

Tom thought the Beast looked desperate, and more hunched than before. He seemed to stagger as he battered people out of his path. He no longer seemed interested in scratching people, only getting past. But where was he heading? Not to the gates, but towards the grand fountain near the middle of the courtyard.

He wants water…

Tom peered closer, using the power of the Golden Helmet. There was something different about Okawa. His scales were drier, even flaking in places. Then Tom noticed that the cavity on top of the Beast's head was almost empty. All at once, Tom remembered how the Beast had stooped to fill it with water at the marshes.

Could it be that he needs to keep it filled to stay strong?

"Don't let him get to the fountain!" he shouted.

A line of soldiers formed up ahead of Okawa. The Beast charged at them, bouncing backwards off their shields. Roaring in anger, he barrelled forward again. This time he broke through, leaving the soldiers on their backs, dazed and moaning.

Let's see if you can get past me, Okawa, thought Tom grimly.

He focused the power of his Golden Leg Armour and sprinted across the courtyard, drawing his sword and blocking Okawa's route to the fountain.

Okawa's yellow eyes glared at him and the Beast lunged. Tom ducked a

sideways swipe from the deadly claws, then sidestepped a vertical rake. He slapped the Beast's arm with the flat of his blade, making Okawa hiss in pain.

"Give up, Okawa," said Tom.

The Beast's lipless mouth split in a smile and his black tongue flickered out. Then he turned and ran from the fountain towards the City walls.

Where's he going? thought Tom.

The answer hit him.

The moat!

If Okawa reached it, he'd be able to replenish his powers. Then he'd be unstoppable.

I mustn't let him reach the water...

Tom's eyes scanned the courtyard and fell on a coil of rope outside the stables. He picked it up, and quickly made a lasso at one end. Okawa was clambering up some stone steps at the outer wall now. Once he reached the top, he could leap into the moat.

Tom sped to the bottom of the steps, swinging the lasso. *Here goes…* He tossed it, just as the Beast was about to jump.

The loop fell over Okawa's head and tightened around his middle. Tom gave the rope a heave and Okawa toppled backwards, bouncing on his shell to the bottom of the steps. The crater in his head had just a few drops of water inside, and the Beast struggled to stand.

"It's over," said Tom.

Okawa rushed at him, taking him by surprise, and slammed his shoulder into Tom's chest. Tom stumbled and tripped, dropping his sword and shield, and the end of the rope. Okawa advanced, claws flexing and slicing through the lasso. A voice came through the ruby in Tom's belt: *You'll be my slave soon.*

Just then Storm reared into view, rearing up on his hind legs and wheeling his front hooves at the Beast, who fell back. Captain Harkman sat astride the stallion, and behind them came Silver.

"Thanks," said Tom, leaping up and patting Storm's flank. He grabbed his sword and shield and turned to face Okawa. It was too late. The Beast had already scrambled back up the steps, and Tom just caught a glimpse of a webbed foot as the Beast jumped off the walls into the water below.

No! Tom thought. *He'll be back to full strength.*

He smelled burning, and glanced

back. The stables were ablaze, with
smoke swirling into the sky and
horses rushing from the flames,
snorting and rearing in panic.

"Someone must have knocked over
a lamp in the panic," said Captain
Harkman. "Soldiers! Bring water!"

"Wait…" said Tom.

Captain Harkman's brow furrowed. *The antidote must be placed in a burning flame.*

"Trust me," said Tom. "We can rebuild the stable block, but we need fire to defeat Okawa."

As soon as Tom spoke, the Beast

rushed through the main gates. His head was spilling over with water again, his scales slick and healthy. He stood tall, almost twice the height he was before.

I need to get him near the flames, thought Tom. *Even if it harms my uncle.*

"Come and face me, if you dare," he called to the Beast.

Okawa's voice filled his head. *This day will be your last, Master of the Beasts!*

"Not if I have anything to do with it," muttered Tom.

CHAPTER SIX

FIGHTING FIRE

Okawa came at him, covering the ground in giant ranging strides.

"Keep Storm and Silver safe," said Tom to Captain Harkman. "And contain the Infected if you can."

"I hope you know what you're doing," said the captain.

So do I, thought Tom.

He ran towards the burning stables, Okawa gaining on him. With screaming people running about everywhere, it was hard to tell who was infected and who wasn't. Tom avoided all of them, focusing only on reaching the fire. If Daltec was right, the flames held the key to defeating Okawa.

I just hope he hurries up with the antidote.

A dozen or so skittish horses from the stables were already outside, frantic but thankfully unhurt.

Tom turned and saw Okawa. With his back to the fire, the heat was intense. "Come closer..." Tom muttered under his breath.

Okawa paused ten paces from him. *He's wary*, thought Tom.

"Are you a coward?" Tom called.

Okawa's yellow eyes glittered, but he didn't step any closer.

Tom saw Daltec emerge from a door across the courtyard. "We have it," yelled the Wizard. He held up a small glass vial containing a clear liquid.

"Throw it to me," Tom shouted back.

Daltec drew back his arm and hurled the vial. It flew through the air, but straight away Tom saw that

the throw hadn't been powerful enough. The vial dipped, arcing straight towards Okawa.

Oh no...

Just as it was about to come into range of the Beast's webbed hand, Daltec brought his hand to his lips and blew. The vial suddenly lifted and floated an extra few paces. Tom jumped up and snatched it from the air. Nearer to the flames, the liquid began to turn purple.

Okawa's throat emitted a low growl.

"I need him closer," Tom said.

"Leave it to us," said Daltec.

He shot out his hands and a bolt of blue light fizzed from his palms, exploding at Okawa's feet in a shower of sparks. The Beast staggered away. The next blast hit Okawa on the shell, shifting him further. Tom could see

the magic wasn't really hurting the Beast, but it was doing the trick. Each bolt Daltec fired drove Okawa nearer to Tom, and the blazing stables. Tom felt the flames licking at the back of his neck, almost unbearable.

He removed the stopper from the vial as Okawa stumbled towards him.

I hope this works. My uncle's in there, somewhere.

He leaped at the Beast, ready to pour the liquid over his shell. But Okawa twisted and his claws whipped through the air. Tom had to weave and back away. He lunged forward again, but the Beast slammed a webbed foot into Tom's chest. He rolled across the ground, and the vial slipped from his fingers.

The antidote!

He scrambled to grab the small bottle. It was only half full, the rest having been spilled in the dust. He plugged the stopper back in. *I can't waste any more.*

Okawa's chest was heaving up and down. *I'm not stupid, Master of the Beasts*, said his voice. *Your uncle is forever lost.*

"We'll see about that," said Tom. Using the power of the Golden Boots, he leaped skyward, over the Beast's head. As he did, he hurled the vial down at Okawa. It smashed, showering the purple liquid over the Beast's shell.

The Beast's pained shriek filled his ears.

Ooof! Something crashed into Tom like an invisible fist, knocking him to the ground. He slid across the cobbles, gasping for breath. When he looked up he saw the old woman from the road to Errinel, standing a few paces away. She wore the same tattered, hooded cloak, but her walking staff was no longer made of gnarled wood. It gleamed silver, and was carved with strange symbols. A sorceress's staff. He had been hit by a magical blast.

The old woman drew back the hood. Red hair fell freely around a terribly familiar face.

"Kensa," Tom gasped. He struggled to stand, but fell back, still winded. To

his dismay, he saw Okawa was still in Beast form. The purple antidote had left deep cracks and scars in his shell, but it obviously hadn't been enough to finish the job.

You've failed, said the Beast in his mind.

As Kensa strode towards him, staff raised, Tom knew it was over.

CHAPTER SEVEN

BROKEN

A bolt of blue light exploded in Kensa's chest, stopping her in her tracks. She looked up and smiled at Daltec, who was raising his hand, ready to release another bolt of magic. "Your mentor Aduro would be ashamed of your efforts, Daltec," she said. "It'll take more than your pathetic magic to stop me."

The end of her staff glowed like

molten lava as she pointed it at Tom.

"This is going to hurt," she said, grinning horribly.

Out of nowhere, a green bolt of light struck the staff, knocking it off target. An orange ray shot from the end like a stream of fire and scorched the ground beside Tom's head.

"What's this?" shrieked Kensa. She gritted her teeth, straining to bring the weapon back to bear on Tom, but the green energy was holding it in place. Tom glanced up and saw not Daltec, but Petra. The green light was shooting from her hands as she approached.

"What are you doing, girl?" said Kensa. "Tom's your enemy!"

"Not today," said Petra. Her arms trembled as she fought Kensa's strength. "Malvel taught me well, don't you think?"

Kensa's eyes shone with rage and she spoke in a growl. "Not. Well. Enough." With a roar she lifted her staff and the orange ray blasted Petra in the chest. The young witch flew through the air and thudded into a wall, sinking to the ground unconscious. Daltec's hand went

to his mouth, fear written over his features. Then his eyes focused on Kensa.

"Don't even think about it," snapped Kensa. At another wave of her staff, Daltec fell backwards, and rolled through an open door. It slammed closed behind him.

"Now, finish the traitor, Okawa," snarled Kensa.

Tom saw the Beast stride towards the prone form of Petra.

He's going to infect her! Tom felt the air stir above him and saw a silver flash as Kensa brought her staff down towards his skull. He rolled aside as the weapon thumped into the ground. "Time for you to die as well," said the sorceress, lifting her staff for another attack.

"Not today," muttered Tom. He

cracked the flat of his blade against
Kensa's knuckles and the witch
dropped her staff with a howl. Tom
turned and saw that Okawa had
almost reached Petra, too far away for
him to help. Her eyes were closed.

There was only one thing he could do to save her. He hurled his sword, which went spinning through the air at Okawa's shell. Too late Tom worried he'd made a terrible mistake. If the blade entered the Beast's body, his uncle would surely die as well.

CRACK!

The hilt slammed right into the centre of the Beast's shell. Fragments broke off and tumbled to the ground, bouncing off Tom's boots as Okawa fell to his knees in front of Petra. The witch stirred, eyes opening in panic as she saw the Beast so close. But Okawa was changing, shrinking before Tom's eyes. With a moan of pain, the Beast rolled sideways and curled into a ball. A fog of sickly yellow seeped up from his body, shrouding him completely. Tom stepped forward, fear eating at his heart.

I've killed him... My uncle is dead.

From inside the yellow smoke, he saw thrashing limbs and heard horrible cries of pain. As he approached, the smoke cleared. And there, in the Beast's place, lay Uncle Henry, snoring loudly.

Looking across the courtyard, Tom saw people were coming to their senses, their eyes returning to their normal colours. Some shook or rubbed their heads, kneeling on the ground. Captain Harkman bellowed orders to his soldiers to form a line from the well and bring buckets of water to the burning stables. Daltec came out of the door, limping as fast as he could to Petra's side.

Kensa, Tom realised, had vanished.

I can deal with her another day.

Tom kneeled next to his uncle and shook his shoulder lightly.

"Not now, Maria," muttered his uncle.

Tom laughed. "It's me, Uncle. We're not in Errinel now."

Henry sat up and rubbed his eyes. "How strong was that punch you

brought me?"

Tom hugged his uncle, then turned to Daltec. "Can you watch him for a moment?"

Daltec nodded as Tom ran off towards the Wizard's chamber. Elenna met him on the stairs with the ropes hanging frayed from her wrists, and Silver at her side. "Silver came to help and gnawed through my bonds," she said. "Is everything all right?"

"It is now," said Tom. "There's a lot to explain."

As they returned to the courtyard together, Tom began to fill Elenna in on what had happened.

"Is that Petra?" asked Elenna, her mouth dropping open.

The young witch was deep in conversation with Daltec. She looked pale, but otherwise unhurt by Kensa's powerful blast.

"She saved my life," said Tom.

Elenna shook her head, as though she couldn't believe it.

The barn was just charred black timbers now, but at least the fire was out.

Daltec and Petra turned to them, smiling. "You two make quite a

team," said Tom. "You should work together more often."

Daltec blushed, and Tom noticed that Petra couldn't meet the Wizard's eye.

Interesting, he thought. *Perhaps we'll be seeing more of Petra from now on.*

"I owe you my thanks," Tom said.

Petra shrugged. "It was nothing,"

she said. "Daltec tells me you saved my life as well."

Tom shrugged back. "It was nothing," he echoed.

"I'm afraid Kensa has escaped," said Captain Harkman, striding over from the stables. "My soldiers followed her to the City gates, but she vanished."

Tom retrieved his sword from the ground and buried it in his scabbard. Okawa was no more; that was the main thing. His uncle was safe and the kingdom was free of the terrible plague.

"Kensa will be back," he said. "Evil never rests."

But while there's blood in my veins, I'll be ready for her.

Tom's Beast Quest
continues in a
thrilling new
series, coming
soon!

Have you read all the books in the
latest Beast Quest series,
THE CURSED DRAGON?
Out now!

FREE
COLLECTOR
CARDS
INSIDE!

Series 14: THE CURSED DRAGON
COLLECT THEM ALL!

Tom must face four terrifying Beasts as he
searches for the ingredients for a potion to
rescue the Cursed Dragon.

978 1 40832 920 7

978 1 40832 921 4

978 1 40832 922 1

978 1 40832 923 8

Win an exclusive
Beast Quest T-shirt and goody bag!

In every Beast Quest book the Beast Quest logo is
hidden in one of the pictures. Find the logo in this book
and make a note of which page it appears on.
Write the page number on a postcard and
send it in to us.
Each month we will draw one winner to receive
a Beast Quest T-shirt and goody bag.

THE BEAST QUEST COMPETITION:
OKAWA THE RIVER BEAST
Orchard Books
338 Euston Road, London NW1 3BH
Australian readers should email:
childrens.books@hachette.com.au

New Zealand readers should write to:
Beast Quest Competition
PO Box 3255, Shortland St, Auckland 1140, NZ.
or email: childrensbooks@hachette.co.nz

Only one entry per child.
Closing date: 31 July 2014

You can also enter this competition
via the Beast Quest website: www.beastquest.co.uk

Fight the Beasts,
Fear the Magic

www.beastquest.co.uk

Have you checked out the Beast Quest website?
It's the place to go for games, downloads, activities,
sneak previews and lots of fun!

You can read all about your favourite beasts,
download free screensavers and desktop wallpapers
for your computer, and even challenge your friends
to a Beast Tournament.

Sign up to the newsletter at www.beastquest.co.uk
to receive exclusive extra content and the
opportunity to enter special members-only
competitions. We'll send you up-to-date info on all
the Beast Quest books, including the next exciting
series which features four brand-new Beasts!

Series 1
COLLECT THEM ALL!

Have you read all the books in Series 1 of
BEAST QUEST? Read on to find out where
it all began in this sneak peek from book 1,
FERNO THE FIRE DRAGON...

FERNO
THE FIRE DRAGON

978 1 84616 483 5

SEPRON
THE SEA SERPENT

978 1 84616 482 8

ARCTA
THE MOUNTAIN GIANT

978 1 84616 484 2

TAGUS
THE HORSE-MAN

978 1 84616 486 6

NANOOK
THE SNOW MONSTER

978 1 84616 485 9

EPOS
THE FLAME BIRD

978 1 84616 487 3

CHAPTER ONE

THE MYSTERIOUS FIRE

Tom stared hard at his enemy. "Surrender, villain!" he cried. "Surrender, or taste my blade!"

He gave the sack of hay a firm blow with the poker. "That's you taken care of," he announced. "One day I'll be the finest swordsman in all of Avantia. Even better than my father, Taladon the Swift!"

Tom felt the ache in his heart that always came when he thought about his father. The uncle and aunt who had brought Tom up since he was a baby never spoke about him or why he had left Tom to their care after Tom's mother had died.

He shoved the poker back into its pack. "One day I'll know the truth," he swore.

As Tom walked back to the village, a sharp smell caught at the back of his throat.

"Smoke!" he thought.

He stopped and looked around. Through the trees to his left, he could hear a faint crackling as a wave of warm air hit him.

Fire!

Tom pushed his way through the trees and burst into a field. The golden wheat had been burned to black stubble and a veil of smoke hung in the air. Tom stared in horror. How had this happened?

He looked up and blinked. For a second he thought he saw a dark shape moving towards the hills in the distance. But then the sky was empty again.

An angry voice called out. "Who's there?"

Through the smoke, Tom saw a figure stamping around the edge of the field.

"Did you come through the woods?" the man demanded. "Did you see who did this?"

Tom shook his head. "I didn't see a soul!"

"There's evil at work here," said the farmer, his eyes flashing. "Go and tell your uncle what's happened. Our village of Errinel is cursed – and maybe all of us with it!"

Read FERNO THE FIRE DRAGON to find out what happens next...